This edition first published 2020

© Copyright D C R James, 2020
ISBN: 978-1-9161952-2-6

Find more by the author at DCRJames.com
Printed by Book Printing UK, PE2 9BF

The Adventures of Bearwolf

By D. C. R. James

With David Roche & Kevin Campbell

The Adventures of Bearwolf

Book One   Bearwolf and Fidget

Book Two   The Bravest Penguineapig

Book Three   The Baldrus Olymbics

Book Four   The Lonely Giraffe

Book Five   Mant VS Grab

Book Six   Professor Yessir's Birthday Machine

Book Seven   The Cruckoo's Napsack

BOOK ONE

1

BEARWOLF AND FIDGET

3

BEARWOLF

Fidget

"A problem for you,
Is a problem for me."

The Predictascope

Bearwolf loves snoozing,

And drinks fizzy pop.

Fidget loves seeing

How high she can hop.

"Bearwolf!" Says Fidget,

"I think you should stop.

Bubble bath's *naughty*

To put in your pop!"

But Bearwolf likes bubbles,

He burps, and they go,

Far out of sight,

Where nobody knows…

Late one morning,

Bearwolf was snoring.

"That's boring!" Said Fidget,

"I'm going exploring!"

Under and over,

Around and behind,

"I wonder," Said Fidget,

"What will I find?"

Then down on the beach,

By an old piece of rope,

Fidget discovered...

A Predictascope!

Fidget looked through it,

And what did she see?

"A very big wave,

And it's coming for me!"

But she put it back down,

And the wave disappeared.

"That's odd!" Said Fidget,

"What's going on here?"

She went and told Bearwolf,

What she had seen.

"Are you sure," Bearwolf yawned,

"That it wasn't a dream?"

"*I* think," Said Fidget,

"It's trying to say,

We must go and explore,

What could make such a wave."

So they packed some fresh clothes,

And some snacks for their tea,

Left a note on their door,

And went down to the beach…

Where Lilow, a turtle,

As big as could be,

Said, "Climb on my back,

And we'll sail the sea."

So together they sailed,

A night and a day,

'Til they came to the Baldrus,

At Kiblubbin Bay.

The Baldrus were

Bellyflopping into the sea,

To hunt at the bottom,

For clams for their tea.

"We used to catch jellyfish,

They were the best.

Don't even like clams,

But there's nothing else left."

So, deeper and deeper,

They needed to dive,

'Til the waves that they made,

Became ever so high.

And through the Predictascope,

Bearwolf could see,

"A problem for you,

Is a problem for me."

So they got back on Lilow,

Pushed off from the beach,

And set sail for the land,

Of the Jellyfish thieves.

But the Jellyfish thieves,

Were just Penguineapigs,

These cute little creatures,

Scared out of their wits.

"Why have you taken

The Baldrus' jellies?"

Said Fidget, "That's mean!

And it's awfully smelly!"

"We needed the jellies,

To use them as bricks,

To build us a wobbly,

Warm pyramid.

We need to keep warm,

Now the dark shadow master

Is blocking the sun,

It gets colder much faster."

Through the Predictascope,

Bearwolf could see,

"A problem for you,

Is a problem for me."

So, though they were tired,

And the journey was long,

The Predictascope said,

That they must carry on.

"Remember the jellies,

The clams, and the waves.

Now it's not just our island,

That we have to save."

So they got back on Lilow,

This time even faster,

They sailed to the land

Of the dark shadow master.

And as they approached,

The dark shadow grew taller,

And Bearwolf and Fidget

Both felt a lot smaller...

But when they arrived,

My how they laughed!

The dark shadow master…

Was just Mr. Giraffe!

"Hey Mr Giraffe,

Your stilts are too long!

When you use them, you block out

Penguineapig's sun!"

"*I*… eat rainbows up in the *sky*,

But now the rainbows are rather *high*,

In fact, the rainbows are almost *gone*,

That's why I need my legs so *long*…*long*…*long*…"

Through the Predictascope,

Bearwolf could see,

"A problem for you,

Is a problem for me."

So they climbed up his shoulders,

And slid down his neck,

And landed on Lilow,

Who asked them, "Where next?"

"To see the Professor,

On the island of facts!"

But when they arrived,

It was covered in cracks.

From overhead,

A loud voice shouted down,

"You there, yes you there,

Best stay off the ground!"

The ground started shaking,

But, just in time,

Down tumbled a rope,

And up, UP they climbed.

"So *you* stole the rainbows!"

Said Fidget out loud.

"Yessir, this Professor,

Must stay off the ground!

It rumbles and shakes

With a terrible sound.

Every building I've built

Ends up falling back down."

Through the Predictascope,

Bearwolf could see,

"A problem for you,

Is a problem for me."

"Time is short," said Professor,

So best not be slow!

Take two of these rainbows

Wherever you go."

So, Bearwolf and Fidget

Clung on really tight,

And with a one, two, three – *whoosh* -

They'd already arrived…

At Mole Island,

A strange, dark place. *Fact.*

Full of moles in holes,

Wearing bowler hats.

"Why are you digging?"

Said Fidget, "It's shaking the ground."

"And what's it to you?"

Said a mole with a frown.

"Well, your digging is causing

All sorts of trouble –

Professor's new buildings

Are turning to rubble,

So he's using rainbows,

To stay off the ground,

So for Mr. Giraffe,

There are none to be found,

So *he's* wearing stilts,

That are bigger than trees,

And his shadow is making

Penguineapigs freeze.

So *they're* stealing jellies,

To build a warm place,

But the jellies are Baldrus'

Favourite taste.

Without jellies, the Baldrus

Must dive really deep,

To get clams that they don't even like

For their tea.

And the waves that they make

Are as big as the sea,

And they're coming straight for us,

Bearwolf, and me.

So, please, Mr Mole,

Don't be mistaken,

It all starts with you,

And your digging and shaking."

The mole said,

"Yes, that may well be true,

But before you accuse,

Pray tell what *you'd* do,

I'd be willing to bet,

That you'd dig some holes too,

If you had to escape from

Them bubbles of *doom*."

"Them bubbles of *doom*?

That sounds really bad.

What kind of a terrible

Monster makes that?"

Looking through the Predictascope,

Bearwolf's jaw dropped.

Who's that,

Pouring bubble bath into his pop?

Then gulping and slurping,

And burping big bubbles!

I think we have found

Who is causing these troubles...

"It's *me*!" Said Bearwolf.

"Who could have guessed,

That blowing those bubbles

Could cause such a mess!"

So Bearwolf said sorry,

And Fidget did too,

"For thinking the start

Of the troubles was you...

And *you* and *you* –

And *you* and *you* –

And *you* and *you* –

And *you* and *you* –

Before in the end,

I saw it was me.

Sometimes our own bubbles

Are the hardest to see."

So they set off on Lilow,

With sleep in their eyes,

To make their way home,

As night filled the sky.

And Bearwolf, he promised,

No more would he blow,

Bubbles of trouble,

Where nobody knows…

BOOK TWO

THE BRAVEST PENGUINEAPIG

Penguineapigs

"Some are born brave,
Some become brave,
And, also, Penguineapigs."

Penguineapig saying

The Penguineapigs live

In constant fear,

Of everyone and everything,

Far and near.

They're scared of the rain,

They're scared of the thunder,

They've even banned beds,

So monsters don't live under.

They're frightened of shadows,

They freeze in the dark,

They've been known to faint,

When they hear a dog bark.

They're spooked out by spiders,

Panicked by bugs,

Afraid of big flowers,

And snails and slugs.

They're scared to be different,

Worried by change,

And most nervous of all,

When things stay the same.

They worry that everything's

Going to go wrong,

The list is just endless,

It goes on and on.

But the one thing that makes

Them all the most scared,

Is the Octopussycat,

Whose island they share.

They've never met her,

But, if they did,

They'd find she's the friendliest

Creature there is.

Sometimes, when she sees them,

She gives them a wave,

And she tries to approach them,

And ask them to play.

But as soon as they see her,

Eight claws in the air,

They stop what they're doing,

And run away elsewhere.

But she won't give up,

She still lives for the day,

When they give her a chance,

And let her join in and play.

The Penguineapigs' names

All start with a P,

Like Pip, Pop, Pat,

Paddy and Pete.

Pete, the Penguineapig,

Was like all the rest.

He wasn't the worst,

And he wasn't the best.

He liked playing violin,

But only second fiddle.

And he liked going swimming,

But only in the middle.

Each day, the Penguineapigs,

Would go for a swim,

And they'd check it was safe,

Before they got in.

They would check to make sure,

No one else was around,

By looking for movement,

Listening for sound.

And when they were sure,

Or, as sure as could be,

They'd get in together,

And swim in the sea.

One day, they were swimming,

At their favourite spot,

In the cove to the north,

Of Seaweedipig Rock.

The water was medium,

The current was weak,

They swam in a huddle,

In the middle was Pete.

Then all of a sudden,

The calm was no more,

As eight claws were spotted,

Waving from the shore.

Instinct took over,

They knew what to do,

They ducked under water,

And counted, slowly, to two.

One and three quarters… Two!

They came up for air.

Success! Octopussycat…

Was no longer there.

But something strange *had* happened,

Something very strange indeed,

Now every single Penguineapig,

Was terrified of *Pete*.

He tried to ask them,

Was it something that he did?

But whenever he approached them,

They all just ran away and hid.

At teatime, they were having tea,

He tried to join in,

But when he went to sit down,

They all ran away from him.

And things only got worse,

As they huddled up for sleep,

When he tried to get his usual spot,

There was no room left for Pete.

Forced to stay up on his own,

At first, Pete froze and cried.

"Why have my friends rejected me?

Why do they run and hide?

Is it something that I said?

Or something that I've done?

I'm still the same, why have they changed?

Why do they hide and run?"

The unfamiliar sounds of night

T-witted and t-wooed.

And, when Pete could cry no more,

At last he knew just what to do.

One step at a time,

He'd keep on counting up to two,

One step, then another step,

That is what he'd do.

At first, he walked in circles,

But he found he preferred squares,

As he felt safer in corners,

And spent a little longer there.

"One. Two. One. Two."

Talking to himself,

He didn't even notice,

When he was joined by someone else.

Then, out of the darkness,

A voice filled Pete with dread,

He breathed and counted up to two,

While this is what it said…

"Hello, I'm Octopussycat,

How do you doodle do?

I'm really quite a friendly cat,

Can I be friends with you?"

At first, Pete's heart,

Beat like a flapping bird,

But he took another big breath,

And listened to the actual words.

And he took another deep breath,

And he counted up to two,

And said, "Yes, I guess, I could try

To be friends with you."

And, after a while,

Pete became more calm,

As he grew less afraid,

Of the cat with eight arms.

And he discovered that there are

Some most wonderful games,

You can play with new friends,

Who *don't* quite look the same.

So they swam and they walked,

And they swapped their best stories,

And they were still talking,

Right into the morning,

And they were still laughing,

When up came the sun,

"Well, doesn't time fly,

When you're having fun!"

When the other Penguineapigs,

Opened their eyes,

Each one nearly fainted,

In total surprise.

So Octo said, "Pete,

My best friend ever made,

I should probably go,

For your friends are afraid."

"But before I go, Pete,

There's one thing you must tell.

Why are you covered in

Seaweed and shells?"

Now Pete understood,

Why his friends had been scared,

He looked like a monster,

With seaweed for hair!

It must have been then,

When he went for a swim,

And he got out to find,

They were all scared of him.

So Pete pulled out the seaweed,

And shook out the shells,

And suddenly he looked

Much more like himself.

And all the Penguineapigs

Saw it was Pete,

"The bravest Penguineapig

There's *ever* been!"

So Pete told them all,

The new stories he knew,

And told them the tale of the night

He'd been through.

And later that day,

When they went for their swim,

They invited Octopussycat,

To come and join in.

And together they swam,

To the edge and to the end,

For they all felt much safer,

Now that they were friends.

BOOK THREE

THE BALDRUS OLYMBICS

The Baldrus

If you make up the rules,
You're more likely to win.

Baldrus Book of Wisdumb

One evening,

Bearwolf was watching the moon,

When a Baldrus went by,

With a fish on a spoon.

He said to the Baldrus,

"Where are you going?"

But the big-headed Baldrus

Showed no signs of slowing.

"Kiblubbin – bla-de-blah,

Bald biscuits!

I'm carrying the torch,

For the Baldrus Olymbics!"

When Bearwolf told Fidget

What he had seen,

Fidget said, "Are you sure,

That it wasn't a dream?"

They went and asked Lilow,

And Lilow explained,

"The Baldrus are having

Their annual games."

So they went to the Baldrus,

And asked to join in.

"Why?" Said the Baldrus,

"There's no chance you'll win."

"Oh please!" Said Fidget,

"We've come all this way"

"Well, all right," Said Baldrus,

"What sborts can you play?

Can you blay belly-flopping?

Can you blay belly-bopping?

Can you blay roly-boly?

Can you blay mud-snorkelling?

Jellyfish juggling? Biggy-back Bolo?

Can you even blay ubsidedown backsliding

Down a slippery hill backwards?

No? Didn't think so!"

"We can leapfrog!" Said Fidget,

But the Baldrus just laughed.

"That's not a real sbort,

Your sborts are just daft!"

So the Baldrus all boasted,

They'd beat all the rest.

"Come and blay with us,

And we'll show you who's best!"

When all had arrived,

The ceremonies got started,

With Baldrus belly bongos,

And some rather wobbly dances.

Then first up was the belly-bopping,

The Baldrus took their stance…

And with bellies that size,

No one else stood a chance.

The professor refused,

To be part of such violence.

And the Penguineapigs fainted,

And lay there in silence.

For the wrestling,

Giraffe didn't fit in the ring,

So the Baldrus all shouted,

"Disqualify him!"

"Kiblubbin!" Said the Baldrus,

"We told you we'd win.

So, what other sborts

Will you be beaten in?"

Next came the six metres,

Mud-snorkelling dash.

The Baldrus came first,

With an almighty SPLASH!

Then jelly-fish munching

Was just before lunch,

And the Baldrus ate all

The competition for brunch.

The Baldrus all boasted,

"We're King of the Waves!"

And the moles almost drowned,

When they got in their way.

In Biggy-back Bolo,

The Baldrus got Gold,

Which had something to do

With the Baldrus-shaped goals.

It's the upside down backslide,

On a slippery hill…

"Oh dear!" Said Giraffe,

"I *do* feel quite ill!"

When all the events

Had come to an end,

The Baldrus had won lots of medals,

But lost lots of friends.

They were boasting and shouting,

How they were so great,

Singing, "Cod save the Baldrus,

We'll never be fish bait!"

So Bearwolf stood up,

And spoke up for the rest.

"At Baldrus games,

Baldrus are bound to be best."

"New games!" Said Fidget.

"We'll each get to choose.

Let's see if the Baldrus

Have fun when they lose!"

So the big day arrived,

And the Baldrus went first.

They chose Belly-boasting,

"We're best and you're… worst!"

It was no great surprise,

When they passed their own test,

And they started to gloat,

"Watch us win all the rest!"

"Time for the high jump!"

Fidget announced.

Before coming first,

With a very big bounce.

"Kiblubbin!" Said the Baldrus,

"That sbort's not fair!

It's not 'cos we lost,

It's just 'cos we don't care."

The Penguineapigs dazzled,

In the synchronised swim,

While the Baldrus attempt,

Was considered rather grim.

"Kiblubbin!" Said the Baldrus,

"That sbort's not fair!

It's not 'cos we lost,

It's just 'cos we don't care."

The Mant chose the relay,

Bearwolf chose darts,

And the moles went for

Dig a big hole in the dark.

"Kiblubbin!" Said the Baldrus,

"That sbort's not fair!

It's not 'cos we lost,

It's just 'cos we don't care."

Then the one hundred metres,

That was up last.

It was won by a neck,

And the neck was Giraffe's.

"Kiblubbin!" Said the Baldrus,

"That sbort's not fair!

It's not 'cos we lost,

It's just 'cos we don't care."

"I'm terribly sorry,

How *rude* of me to win."

Said Mr Giraffe,

With a rainbow-sized grin.

By the time it got dark,

They were all very tired,

So they cooked a big feast,

And they sat round the fire.

But the Baldrus were sulking,

Still sat on their own,

In the corner, all grumpy,

And having a moan.

"Kiblubbin!" Moaned the Baldrus,

"Life isn't fair!

If we can't be the best,

Then why should we care?"

Bearwolf stood up,

And said, "Baldrus, my friends,

Come and eat with us,

Now that the sport's at an end.

We've all won and lost,

Tried and failed again,

But once it's all over,

Let's remember we're friends.

Each of us is our own gift

To the games,

If the losers don't lose,

Winning's not quite the same.

If you must be a winner,

Compete with yourself,

Don't get stuck in comparing,

With everyone else.

In the end it's like breakfast,

And lunch and dinner,

It's the eating together,

That makes us all winners."

"Kiblubbin!" Said the Baldrus,

And then they all laughed,

When the biggest, boastiest Baldrus

Let out a big Baldrussy fart.

"Well, we are pretty hungry!"

They said to each other,

So they joined in the feast,

And they all sat together.

And when they had finished,

They went home with their medals,

Of silver seashells,

And bright green emeralds,

And the great memories,

From a wonderful day,

Of the friends that they'd seen,

And the games that they played.

And Bearwolf said,

"That was a wonderful feast."

And Fidget said,

"You made a wonderful speech."

And the Baldrus,

Well, they'd learnt a valuable thing,

If you make up the rules,

You're more likely to win.

BOOK FOUR

THE LONELY GIRAFFE

Mr.Giraffe

Mr Giraffe

Was tall and polite.

He ate rainbows by day,

And wrote poems by night.

Yes, he was a poet,

His head in the clouds,

He loved to make poems,

And say them out loud.

"Red, orange, yellow,

Green and blue...

Indigo, violet,

I think I love you!"

Yes, he loved saying poems,

But one thing was missing,

He never had anyone

With him to listen.

When Bearwolf and Fidget

Heard he was alone,

They said, "Come and stay with us,

Here at our home."

So he packed up some rainbows,

In an elephant's nose,

And he walked through the ocean,

On the tips of his toes.

And when he arrived,

To stay with his friends,

Mr Giraffe,

He was happy again!

He read Bearwolf poems,

To send him to sleep,

While Fidget, she hipped,

And she hopped to the beat.

Then, one day, when Fidget said,

"Let's go exploring!"

Giraffe said, "Ok, then!"

So as not to be boring.

But he got tangled up,

In a terrible mess,

And he couldn't write poems,

Because of the stress.

"Oh deary me!"

Said Giraffe on his knees,

"I think that this island,

Just isn't for me."

So he packed up his rainbows,

And walked through the sea,

To Mant Island,

Where no one was ever lonely.

He helped build a tower,

Up to the sky,

And the Mant said they'd never

Built something so high.

Then, by mistake,

Giraffe knocked it back down,

And it fell from the sky,

All the way to the ground.

"I'm dreadfully sorry!"

Said Mr Giraffe.

"How terribly clumsy,

How terribly daft!"

But the Mant were upset,

And not at all pleased,

"Mr Giraffe, you must leave,

You *must* leave!"

So he went to the Baldrus,

Who were swimming backstroke,

And he tried to fit in,

And he laughed at their jokes.

But Baldrus eat jellyfish,

By the double dozen,

And they all greet each other,

With the strange word "Kiblubbin".

"Kiblubbin?" He thought,

"What a wobbly word!

They're the silliest creatures,

That I've ever heard."

So, though not alone,

He did not feel better,

And decided to write

The Penguineapigs a letter.

"Dear Penguineapigs,

I hope you are well,

I like writing poetry,

As you can tell.

Would you mind very much,

If I were to stay?

I won't be much trouble,

I'll keep out of your way."

But when he arrived,

They could not be seen.

So he tried to settle in,

And he kept the place clean,

But soon he grew weary,

Where had they all gone?

He looked high and low,

But he could not find one.

Then, one day, he saw them,

Hiding down by the beach.

"Oh dear." He thought,

"Are they hiding from me?"

So he walked shyly over,

To try to make friends,

But before he could get there,

They'd all hidden again.

"Lonely, it may be,

To live on my own,

But it's worse when they run off,

And leave me alone."

So, searching again,

For a temporary home,

He asked the Professor,

But Yessir said "No!"

Now he only had one place,

That he *could* go,

So he went to the moles,

With his head hanging low.

The Moles, digging holes, said,

"Stay for the night.

We could use your left leg,

As a measuring device."

But in the mole hole,

His long legs got stuck,

So along came Professor,

With a crane and a truck.

"Thank you, Professor,

For helping me out.

If I can *ever* repay you,

Just give me a shout."

Professor said, "Well,

There's one thing you could do.

You could help me discover

A planet or two."

So, Mr Giraffe

Went with the Professor,

And they started to build

A megascope together.

Then, for seventeen nights,

They studied the sky,

And found out that the moon

Was a cat in disguise.

And that some of the stars

Could get quite lonely too,

Because during the day,

They had nothing to do.

"Mr Professor,

It's been seventeen days.

Do you think I might read you

The poem I made?"

"I don't much like poems,

I'm sorry to say,

So I'll carry on working,

But you read away."

So, Mr Giraffe

Had a look through his notes,

Found a poem for Professor,

Cleared his throat, and then spoke…

As soon as Professor

Had heard the first line,

He stopped working, and turned,

With a tear in his eye.

The poem was so sad,

It made the clouds weep.

It was too sad to ever,

Ever repeat.

When the poem was finished,

Professor said, "More!"

And Mr Giraffe

Almost fell to the floor.

No one had ever,

Ever asked him for more.

"Are you certain, Professor,

I'm not being a bore?"

"Not at all," Said Professor.

"I've been so unkind.

I can see, you just need,

To say what's on your mind.

I'll stop searching for planets,

Night after night,

And I'll take much more care,

Of the friends by my side."

"Thank you!" Said Giraffe,

Tears blurring his sight,

"Let's do poems by day,

And hunt planets by night!"

So, the next night together,

They both watched the sky,

Until all of a sudden,

Professor said, "My *MY*!"

Suddenly, out through the mists,

They both saw,

Two ears, and a head,

And a chin… and a jaw…

"My gosh," Said Professor,

With a hearty old laugh,

"It's *only* the lost planet,

Of the lonely Giraffe!

This planet's the planet,

All planet-seekers seek!

The very same one,

Of which ancient rhymes speak!"

Now, Mr Giraffe

Had new hope in his eyes,

"If only…" He said,

"Giraffes knew how to fly."

It was then that Professor

Knew just what to do,

He said, "We'll build a space craft,

Designed just for you."

And they came from afar,

And they came from a-wide,

To help build this space craft,

To send through the skies.

The moles mined for metals,

The Mant did the spec,

The Baldrus did lifting,

Even Bearwolf broke sweat.

Fidget revved up the engine,

And tested the alarm,

The Penguineapigs helped

To keep everyone calm.

And in next to no time,

They'd built a huge craft,

That was covered in feathers,

And shaped like giraffe.

When Mr Giraffe

Saw the work was complete,

He said, "You're the best friends,

That there *ever* could be!

I hope you don't mind,

That I'm choosing to go,

But my heart says that somewhere,

Above the rainbow...

There's a lonely Giraffe,

Who is waiting for me,

And I *am* sad to go,

But I *must* go and see."

"But," He said,

"Now that I'm going to leave.

There are some of my things,

That I'll no longer need."

"You may have heard tell,

Of a poem that's told,

That says rainbows all end,

In a big pot of gold."

And with that he produced

A big pot of gold,

And in it were gifts,

All made out of rainbows.

He gave rainjuice to Bearwolf,

Bowties to the moles,

Rainbow scarves to the Penguineapigs,

To keep out the cold.

He had something for everyone

Who'd been there to help,

And to Professor,

He gave the big pot of gold itself.

And carved on the pot,

In the most beautiful letters,

Were the words of this poem,

Which they all read together.

Then he climbed in the space craft,

And said his goodbyes,

And he blasted off,

Full of hope, into the skies.

BOOK FIVE

MANT VS GRAB

"MANT for ALL,
And ALL for MANT!"

Mant Mantra

Careful where you tread,

It's the land of the Mant.

They act just like humans,

But they look just like ants.

The Mant work for one,

And the Mant work for all.

Together they're big,

On their own they are small.

The Mant build so quickly,

They've run out of land.

So now they must find,

A new place to expand.

But the islands were taken,

And nowhere was free,

And the only place left,

Was under the sea.

So, the cleverest Mant,

Were called to the Queen,

Who said, "Build me a big,

Spotty Mant submarine!"

So they did, and they dived,

Down, down in the deep,

And discovered an ocean,

Of space in the sea.

They built New Atmantis,

In no time at all,

An undersea city,

With big fortress walls.

But when they moved in,

To their newly found home,

It soon turned out,

That the Mant weren't alone…

If you ever meet a Grab,

You best watch your nose,

They'll steal your socks,

From right under your toes.

Yes, the Grabs love pinching,

And stealing and nicking,

Robbing and grabbing,

Thieving and tricking.

The Grabs are all cunning,

They lurk in their hide-aways.

When they don't have a sea-horse,

They have to move side-aways.

One day, the Mant,

They all got in a row,

For some of their gloves,

Had gone missing somehow.

Mant A to Mant B said,

"I didn't use them!"

Mant B to Mant A said,

"Well I didn't lose them!"

A pencil, an odd sock,

A bundle of keys…

One day a young Mant

Came home with no knees!

An ice-cream mant,

Who was walking alone,

Was attacked by two Grabs,

Who stole all his cones.

Then a bucket went missing,

Then a submarine door,

Until all that was left,

Was a line on the floor.

"It must be those Grabs,

We've seen them about.

We've got to do something,

To keep those Grabs out!"

So the Mant built a wall,

As high as a kite,

But the Grabs just went round it

That very same night.

"If we can't keep them out,

We'll have to fight back.

One Mant for all!

Now it's time to attack!"

So the Mant made machines,

To spray juice in the sea,

To slow down the Grabs,

And make them all sticky.

So the Grabs got together,

And made their own plan,

To pump brussel sprout soup,

Back up onto the land.

The Mant were so angry,
They laid out some traps.
They caught twenty-five claws,
But not one single Grab.

So the Mant all rushed out,
With nets and long forks,
To hunt down the Grabs,
But they couldn't be caught.

When the Mant got back home,
There was serious trouble -
The Grabs must have pinched
All their oxygen bubbles.

Then the Grab made a sign,

Which said "Mant go away!"

And the Mant made a bigger one,

"NO! WE'RE HERE TO STAY"

The Mant were left shaking,

Their six fists in rage,

So they made up a plan,

To trap Grabs in a cage.

"In the cage we'll put treasures,

Like they've never seen,

Then we'll watch from the safety,

Of our Mant submarine."

So, in the middle,

Of the next sneaky night,

The Grabs shuffled in,

Side by side by side.

"Got you!" The Mant shouted,

And turned on the lights.

"Caught you red-handed!

Now give up the fight!"

So the Mant gave the Grab

A huge telling-off,

From the safety of their submarine,

Which was locked.

But the Mant's faces dropped,

The moment they saw,

The submarine key,

Was in a Grab's claw.

So both sides were trapped,

In a cage of their own.

The Mant couldn't get out,

The Grabs couldn't go home.

The Mant said, "Say sorry,

And we'll leave it at that."

The Grab said, "Say sorry?

You lot must be mad!"

"Well, you stole from us
Without giving it back!"
"Well, we just did that
So you wouldn't attack!"

"You came down here,
And took all our land!"
"Before we came down here,
All this was just sand!"

So backwards and forwards,
The arguments raged,
They shouted all night,
And blew raspberries all day.

Then someone called out,

"We can't let this go on!

We must get to the bottom,

To work out who is wrong!"

But each side was sure,

That the others had started it.

The Mant thought the Grab had,

The Grab thought the Mant did.

"Maybe we're both right,

Maybe we're both wrong!"

Said one Mant before suddenly

Bursting into song.

This Mant sang a song,

That he'd heard the Grab sing,

And after a while,

Both sides joined in.

They sang for themselves,

And they sang for each other.

They sang louder and louder,

Like a chorus of brothers.

When it ended, they clapped,

And they laughed, and they joked,

And they realised that, maybe,

They'd started it both.

So, the Grab reached on over,

And set the Mant free,

And the Mant freed the Grab,

And they both shared the sea.

And whenever they started

To get in a fight,

They sang songs instead,

And it turned out all right.

BOOK SIX

PROFESSOR YESSIR'S BIRTHDAY MACHINE

Professor Yessir

For three hundred and sixty-five,

Days of the year,

The Professor was working,

That much was clear.

Outside his garage,

A sign on display

Said, "Probably busy.

Keep out of my way!"

It's not that he didn't

Like anyone else,

It's just that he found

He worked best by himself.

And people were such
Unpredictable things,
He preferred to converse,
With machines that went 'ping'.

But every 4 years,
A machine would go 'pong',
And he'd stand on his head,
To work out what was wrong.

And then he'd remember,
"Oh yes, silly me!
It must be the twenty-ninth
Of February."

For those who like presents,

By far the worst day,

You could be so unlucky,

To have your birthday.

But Professor was not one

For presents or cake.

He just liked to show off,

All the things that he'd made.

So he'd sent invitations,

To all that he knew,

"Come press lots of buttons,

And see what they do!"

Well everyone came,

And they had lots of fun,

And they marvelled at all,

Of the things that he'd done.

There were black buttons,

Green buttons, Yellow and blue,

There was even a button

For "Fly to the moon!"

And every four years,

It became a tradition,

To go to Professor's

Great Exhibition.

And Fidget, especially,

Just couldn't wait,

She'd stay up all night,

So as not to be late.

But one year the invite,

Just didn't arrive.

"That's odd" Said Fidget,

"I hope he's all right."

So Fidget suggested,

They both go along,

To see the Professor,

And find out what was wrong.

So they went to his island,

But to their surprise,

It seemed everyone else,

Had already arrived.

"Oh *no*." Said Fidget,

"Just look at that queue.

Why weren't we invited?

That's jolly rude!"

Bearwolf said,

"Maybe our invite got lost,

And he is quite forgetful,

Perhaps he forgot."

Fidget was worried,

They'd run out of time,

To press all the buttons,

And go on the rides.

So they joined in the queue,

Right at the back,

And played some i-spy,

And snacked on some snacks…

It seemed to take ages,

But they came to the gate,

And when they got in,

It was all worth the wait!

This was the greatest,

Of Great Exhibitions,

With self-driving horses,

And huge televisions.

There were robots and vehicles,

And chairs that could walk.

There was pop that stayed fizzy,

And plants that could talk.

Bearwolf had a snooze,

In a hat with a screen,

That meant anyone watching,

Could follow his dreams.

The best thing for Fidget,

Was a huge trampoline,

Perfect for down-bouncing,

Into the sea.

At the rainbow pop stand,

They found Mr. Giraffe,

And when he said, "Kiblubbin!"

Well, that made them laugh!

In the bumper-car queue,

A Penguineapig pushed in.

"That's strange!" Said Bearwolf,

"That's not like him."

And the moles were all dancing,

And having a laugh,

And the Mant only said things

That rhymed with giraffe.

The Baldrus were all

Being strangely polite.

"Fidget," Said Bearwolf,

"Something's not right."

"Let's find the Professor,

Perhaps he can say,

Why everyone's acting

So strangely today."

He lived in a tower,

Right up at the top.

So they got in the lift,

And went all the way up…

In through the doorway,

Down a long hall,

The sight that they saw,

Was the strangest of all.

The Professor and friends,

All joking and laughing,

And having what *looked* like,

The best *ever* birthday party.

Another door opened,

And Bearwolf's jaw dropped,

As what *looked* like Bearwolf,

Came in with some pop.

And, just behind

Bearwolf number two,

Was what *looked* like Fidget,

Singing "Happy Birthday to You!"

"That's not Fidget," Said Fidget.

"How can that be?"

"That's not Bearwolf." Said Bearwolf,

"Bearwolf is me."

"And we both know Professor,

He doesn't like cake."

"Stop!" They both shouted,

"This birthday is fake!"

Everything went silent.

No one made a sound.

Slowly, the Professor's

Grey head turned around...

Then CREAK croaked a door,

And out went the light,

And a voice from behind,

Gave them both a big fright.

"Bearwolf! Fidget!

Don't be afraid!

These are just some new versions

Of you that I made.

And a version of me,

That *enjoys* my birthday,

And the singing and laughing,

And fizzy pop cake.

I knew if I made,

A big birthday machine,

I could keep working,

And you'd all be free,

To have a big party,

And eat fizzy cake,

Without me being grumpy,

And spoiling the day."

"But, Professor!" Said Fidget,

"I'm the me that is real,

You forgot to invite me!

How d'you think that *that* feels?

And what does the best

Birthday party even mean,

If you're really just alone,

In a birthday machine?"

The Professor computed

What Fidget had said,

And after a very long

Scratch of his head...

He said, "Yes Sir, you're right!

I've made a mistake,

There's no point being happy,

If the happy is fake!

Let's send out some invites,

Before it's too late,

We'll be real friends,

And I'll grumble about cake!"

So everyone came,

And they sang and had fun,

And Professor showed them,

All the versions he'd done.

And they all thought *how clever*,

But they also agreed,

Though it's good to be perfect,

It's better to be real.

BOOK SEVEN

BEARWOLF
AND THE CRUCKOO'S NAPSACK

There's a bird who's too lazy,
To build his own nest,
A Cruckoo with black and white
Stripes on his chest.

He takes a napsack,
Wherever he goes,
And the napsack is full
Of golden brown slotatoes.

One day this Cruckoo,
Arrived on the beach.
Fidget was exploring,
Bearwolf was asleep.

The Cruckoo said,

"What are you exploring for?"

And Fidget replied,

"So as not to be bored!"

The Cruckoo said,

"Boredom? Well, I have the cure.

Look in my napsack,

You'll need look no more."

So Fidget hopped over,

And had a good look.

"By the way," Said the Cruckoo,

"You can just call me Crook."

166

"Wow!" Said Fidget,

"Never seen these before."

"Take one," Said Cruckoo,

"In fact, take three or four."

So Fidget took three,

And said thanks very much,

And was going to show Bearwolf,

But, Crook said, "Why rush?"

"You *found* the slotatoes,

Why don't you *try* one?

They're ever so tasty,

And nothing's as fun."

So Fidget took the smallest,

And started to nibble,

And as soon as she swallowed,

She started to giggle.

"My golly!" She said,

"They taste ever so strange!

It must be like this,

To have rainbows for brains!

Exploring is boring,

Why couldn't I see?

I used to explore,

Now the world explores me."

168

"Oooh…" She said,

"Now everything's gone slow."

"Don't worry." Said Cruckoo,

"That's just slotatoes."

But Fidget was already

Deep, deep asleep,

And the Cruckoo flew off,

"I'll see you next week!"

It was three days and nights,

Until Bearwolf got up,

Because, usually,

Fidget was his alarm clock.

"I don't think I've ever

Napped for so long."

Said Bearwolf,

"I wonder what *is* going on?"

He tried to wake Fidget,

But he had no luck.

In the land of the nappers,

Fidget was stuck.

He shouted out loudly,

He sprayed her with pop,

But Fidget was napping,

And she just wouldn't stop.

Bearwolf went to see Lilow,

To cross over the sea.

Lilow snored as he floated,

Sleepy as could be.

The Mant were all sunbathing,

Snoozing away.

"Not like them," thought Bearwolf,

"To take Mant holidays."

"Perhaps Baldrus," He thought,

"Can help me instead?"

But he got to their island,

To find them *all* still in bed.

The Penguineapigs were dozing,

All in a big pile,

And Giraffe was asleep,

With a rainbow-sized smile.

For a moment it seemed,

Professor was awake,

But it turned out to be,

Just a robot he'd made.

So, back onto Lilow,

Bearwolf went home,

But with Fidget still napping,

He felt all alone.

Then with a flap,

And a squawk from the blue,

A bird landed next to him…

It was *Cruckoo*.

"Not napping?" He crowed.

"I can help you with that."

Bearwolf said, "For the first time,

I don't want a nap."

"Not nap? Not Nap?

Why's that? Why's that?

Why not explore?

Find out what's in my sack!"

But Bearwolf said,

"I'm not really one for exploring.

If you must know,

I find the whole thing a bit boring.

I would say ask Fidget,

But Fidget is snoring.

Perhaps *you* know why

No one got up this morning?"

"You worry too much!"

Said Cruckoo, with a cluck.

"Eat one of these,

It will bring you good luck."

But before he could eat it,

Fidget crawled over,

And grabbed it, and ate it,

Before falling over.

"That's odd." Said Bearwolf,

"To not say hello.

Must be *some*thing to do with

Your slotatoes."

The Cruckoo said, "Eat one.

It really won't hurt!"

But Bearwolf replied,

"I think *you* should go first!"

175

Cruckoo went pale,

And then he went red,

"I'll have one later,

You go first," He said.

But Bearwolf insisted,

And Cruckoo was scared,

So he took a big bite,

And dozed off right there.

"Hmm..." said Bearwolf,

"I thought that might happen.

These golden slotatoes

Are causing this napping."

So he went to each island,

And left them a note,

"Slotatoes at Bearwolf's"

Is all that he wrote.

Then, while he was waiting,

For them to wake up,

He did a few chores,

To make sure he stayed up.

So he farmed for the Mant,

And he fished for the Baldrus,

And moved the Penguineapigs,

To the place they'd be warmest.

He wound up clocks for Professor,

And before it got dark,

He gathered some rainbows,

For Mr. Giraffe.

He dug for the moles,

To keep them on schedule,

And made Fidget a map,

Of her three favourite cesspools.

He went back to the beach,

And he lay in the sun,

And the creatures woke up,

And turned up, one by one.

They *demanded* slotatoes.

Bearwolf said they were bad.

But they just wouldn't listen,

They thought *he* was mad.

Then Cruckoo woke up,

And blinked in the sun,

And he got rather scared,

When he saw everyone.

"Slotatoes!" They cried,

"Give us all that you have!"

"No! Remember!" Said Bearwolf,

"Slotatoes are bad!"

Cruckoo said, "I've got some,

But you'll all have to pay.

I want free food for life,

And a nice nest to stay."

The Mant said, "Take our food,

Drink Bearwolf's fizz!

We must Give unto Cruckoo,

All that is his!"

So they queued up with gifts,

In return to be fed,

With a single slotato,

That would send them to bed.

"All my life," Bearwolf said,

"I've been the napper!

Giraffe has caught rainbows,

Fidget's been the flapper…

Professor invented,

Penguineapigs got alarmed,

Baldrus ate jellies,

While the Mant farmed their farms.

Now, the napper,

Is each one of you,

And it's left up to me,

To do things *you* should do.

I'm a rainbow-flapping,

Jelly-farmed alarm,

And I am…

Exhausted!"

But nobody listened,

They fought in the queue,

And Bearwolf thought,

"*What* am I going to do?"

Now Lilow had woken,

But all on his own,

He'd spent two whole days,

Without slotatoes.

He had turned a bit pink,

But his memory was back,

So he crawled up to warn them,

To stay off the snack.

But they would not listen,

Not even to him,

So he said to Bearwolf,

"We *must* do something!"

So he made a plan, and said,

"Crook! Serve *me* first,

I'll give you *ten* times,

What you deserve!"

Because Crook was greedy,

He couldn't say no,

So he gave his whole napsack

To brave old Lilow.

Lilow said to the rest,

"You'll all be ok,

Just might be quite owwie,

For one or two days!"

And with that Lilow emptied,

The slotatoes out,

Into the ocean,

Not into his mouth.

"Ten times!" Said Cruckoo,
"I want payment of something!"
"Ten times what you deserve,"
Said Lilow, "Is nothing!"

Now, not only did Cruckoo
Have nothing to sell,
But the slotato eaters
Were angry as well.

So he had to leave fast,
With nowhere to go,
And he went off to live,
A sad life on his own.

The owwies turned to naps,

Daydreams and dawdles,

And a few days later,

Things got back to normal.

The Mant went back to farming,

Giraffe to his sky,

The Penguineapigs to nervousness,

Professor to his whats and whys,

The Baldrus to boasting,

And eating jellies,

Fidget to her new map,

Of cesspools one, two and three.

And everyone laughed,

About what they'd all done,

How could anyone, but Bearwolf,

Find napping such fun?

So they thanked him with gifts,

For all his hard work,

And he had the best nap,

That he'd ever earnt.

And he dreamed of the bubbles,

That he used to blow,

Far out of sight,

Where nobody knows…